The Whiskey Whispered

AMAL MOHAN

notionpress.com

INDIA • SINGAPORE • MALAYSIA

ISBN 979-8-88733-628-2

CONTENTS

MERAKI – A Paroxysm of Memories

It's been five days in a row that I've been stuck in bed with the blues. Pain, medication and boredom have taken their toll. I never knew injuring my vertebral disc, incapacitating my back, would take me back to memories of the past. Haruki Murakami said, "Memories warm you up from inside but they also tear you apart." My memories are filled with gut-wrenching episodes which deserve to be retrieved numerous times.

Close to sixteen years have passed by; everything seems to be forgotten; many run-of-the-mill memories of day-to-day life have faded into oblivion. Countless experiences have been erased and overwritten in the book of memories, but some memories are still vivid. The worst part of holding on to memories is not the pain they rekindle but the urge they provoke to share them with someone. Unhappiness is such a strong element which never lets you forget incidents engraved in your squishy brain.

I was chatting over a cup of coffee in a small restaurant with an old school friend whom I had met accidentally after several years. In those days, mobile phones were rare. I was meddling with my Nokia 3210 while talking to him. I was preoccupied and engrossed in some random thoughts. I heard nothing my friend said. He sounded like a nitwit. I was engulfed with the lone thought of a decade-old love on the verge of coming to an end with her wedding reception that evening. Every single second I felt tears rolling down my face. Being a man, it is difficult to show real emotion. My heart was broken and shattered. There was nothing left for me in this world at that moment.

I just wore a plastic smile and showed no signs of despair. I was composed and patiently lent my ears to my friend. He had had open-heart surgery; the clicking sound of his artificial valve was audible in the silent restaurant. He had his own doubts about tying the knot. The monophonic ringtone of the Nokia mobile screamed for attention. I was lost with a broken heart, wondering if there was any open-heart surgery to set right things, though my knowledge told me that emotions were just an orchestration of the neuro-chemical conglomeration within the hidden regions of grey matter. But, my heart failed to comprehend it. Annoyed, I attended the phone call just to put an end to the rasping sound of the ringtone; it was my father on the other end.

I heard my father say in a brittle voice that my cousin, who was in Grade Ten, had attempted suicide. I was blank. I said, "It is just an attempt, isn't it?" I never knew that a girl of such calibre would have the guts to attempt to kill herself. Who knew, sometimes youth does not provide one with the necessary faculties to handle emotional trauma. In a staccato voice, he announced that she was no more. I was unable to feel the loss, as my pain was more colossal than my cousin's death.

I was inanimate; I just picked up my belongings and left the restaurant without even bothering to say goodbye to my friend. I navigated through the thick traffic with an onslaught of thoughts vacillating in my head. I parked my bike for a while and tried calling my ex-girlfriend who was at her wedding reception. I had promised to attend the celebration. It was a mutual, painful, deliberate decision taken before parting ways. I called to tell that I wouldn't be able to keep my promise. To my disappointment, someone else picked up the call and reluctantly informed me that she wasn't there.

I entered a congested street flanked by low-income housing; dilapidated buildings stood tall; the area looked like a breeding ground for diseases. The pathetic conditions revealed the real faces of low socio-economic families in Chennai. I could see children playing on the streets; some were bare-bodied and dirty. Profanities were a part of their daily life. I could see women doing their daily chores on the street. The stink of the open sewage filled the air. Plastic water pots lay piled up on the streets, waiting to be filled with water from the corporation tank. I was insentient; I could hear or feel nothing. I walked through a narrow stairway leading to the second floor. I could feel the crescendo of misery. I slowly sensed the sound of reality; I could hear the whimper by now.

I saw my 13-year-old cousin lying motionless on the floor. Tears started rolling down my cheeks uncontrollably. I sat near her, held her and lamented. Her pulse must have stopped long before; her body was freezing cold. Time passed by. The body was recovered by the local police for an autopsy since it was an unnatural death. It was already 4:00 p.m. I waited along with the others at the morgue to receive the body.

My mobile phone rang; it was a familiar number. My ex-girlfriend was calling. Her voice sounded painful. "Did you call me?" she asked.

I could hear her breath getting stuck in her throat. "Yes, I wanted to inform you that I won't be able to make it for your wedding reception," I said. There was a period of silence. I heard her sobbing but was unable to console her. I told her that my cousin was no more and asked her to take care and hung up. Sometimes, it is better to settle things abruptly when words don't do you any justice. I burst out crying. I didn't know why I was crying. Was it for the loss of a 13-year-old child or a ten-year relationship? The world seemed strange to me; I could feel a vacuum. At this moment, I wished the world would be annihilated.

The cremation was planned for the next evening, at 4:00 p.m. It was a sleepless night, spent gazing at the lifeless body of the innocent girl. My thoughts were haunted by memories of my ex-girlfriend. The uncertainty of life with the death of my cousin didn't bother me. I still wondered whether destiny substantiated Murphy's Law. Sometimes, intense pain overshadows the lesser troubles. I never knew whether this untimely death had some purpose in my life.

I felt sluggish without any sleep. I was shabbily dressed, with a three-month-old beard and looked scruffy. Something struck me. I wanted to attend my ex-girlfriend's wedding the next morning.

Grief had overwhelmed me completely. It was like a bad dream which could not be shaken off.

At 6:00 a.m. the following morning, I telephoned one of my confidantes and requested him to accompany me to the wedding. I had bought a gift for her and I wanted her to wear it. I went to a saloon, clean-shaved my beard and packed a suit. My friend drove me to his work place. I took a shower there, wore my suit and we both left for the wedding. I rode pillion. My friend tailgated vehicles in the front. Nothing bothered me. Tears continuously rolled down my cheeks. The wedding venue was fifteen kilometres away. The whole ride was like a horrible dream. Not a single second was spared. Ten years of our relationship and our mutual parting for the sake of society and family on her side, flashed before my eyes like a sequence in a Tamil film. I felt like my head was immersed in a bucket of ice-cold water, where I felt suffocated and agonized to hear the external world. I craved for my heart to fall apart and stop beating.

Is love worth all this pain? Is love really this eternal feeling? Is love the best way to find your soul mate? They say, love is temporary insanity cured by marriage. But how many of us are lucky enough to get married to the person we love? Destiny doesn't spare anyone. We just pretend to be happy, accepting whatever happens. Even time doesn't heal certain kinds of pain.

The bike came to a screeching halt. We were near the wedding hall. My eyes were swollen and blood red. The tears hadn't stopped yet. I went to a deli on the street corner, bought a water bottle and splashed the water on my face before entering the wedding hall. I was deaf to the cacophony of the street sounds and the people at the wedding. I was numb and dead inside.

There was no one there who flashed a warm smile; we were uninvited guests. We were gazed at like insects to be stamped to death at any second. But what can they do to a person who is already dead inside.

The ceremonious *getti mellam* was not there. It was a so called Tamil reformation marriage. These reformations are for the sake of their convenience. Even today, people aren't ready to shed their caste and creed. This delusion society suffers from will never change. Society will continue to kill people in the name of honour, to break relationships for their own selfish reasons. Humans have forgotten that we all hail from the same primordial soup and every single species carries the same DNA in their immortal coils.

I felt someone holding my arms; it was her mother, the only person in the whole crowd who was selfless and felt helpless too. She asked me why I was late? I didn't have an answer. She guided me through the crowds to the stage where the married couple was being greeted by friends and family. There she was, my ex-girlfriend, standing as the wife of some other man. Our eyes met without emotion. They couldn't emote due to social apprehensions. A few moments of silence. This silence had lots of stories to tell and pain to share. Tears were a mere expression of all the pain, but its reserves had been exhausted. My heart skipped a beat. I would simply collapse if I stayed there any further. This would inconvenience everybody.

I felt everything freeze around me. There were no words to exchange. What would I wish the person with whom I had wanted to spend the rest of my life with? I handed the gift to her mother and my eyes parted to say one last goodbye to her.

There was a body waiting to be cremated...

TROUVAILLE – The Untold Story of a Lassie

Every creator's dream is to have a fan who appreciates, admires and criticizes his work. Most often, you never get that lucky chance to have one such aficionado. There are people who applaud you in person. Some are Facebook *like* click addicts, some are silent followers and then there are a few sycophants.

While I forage for an ardent fan, the story goes like this...

The day was January 26, 2017, an ordinary day except for it being Republic Day, a government holiday. It was a high-rise apartment in the concrete jungle of busy Chennai. Her bedroom was a little-bitty universe decorated with wall decals. One such poster was of a babyish minion with a quote: I'm not lazy, I'm just on energy-saving mode. Her bed was a mess. There was Chetan Bhagat's *One Indian Girl,* Paulo Coelho's *Brida* and a few other books on her bed. *Brida* was left half open with a doodle on the verso.

She was stupefied by sleep; her mobile alarm had snoozed umpteen number of times. She never knew what awaited her. Her mother cuddled her and offered to bring her coffee in bed as she was on her period. She usually stayed composed to avoid outbursts. She woke up and walked to the main door to pick up the daily newspaper. She started yelling that the paper boy had delivered the wrong newspaper. Instead of *The Hindu* she had received *The New Indian Express*. She wasn't a news addict; science and art columns were what spiked her interest.

With vexation, she leafed through the pages of *The New Indian Express*. The headlines read *Unsung Heroes Adorn Padma Awards* and *Mallya Restrained the Trading Insecurities Markets*. This news sounded mind-numbing to her. She was hunting for some feel good entertainment column in a newspaper unfamiliar to her. She found the *Chennai Express* to be engaging. When she flipped through the fourth page, something grabbed her attention. There was a write-up by Gokul Nair titled *Broken Bridge is a Perfect Hideout.*

It was about an artist, with an uncommon name, who was an autodidact. His primary interests were abstracts and semi abstracts which portrayed feminism, misogyny, violence against women and the power of the female form. He also happened to be a healthcare professional and a researcher. She felt that this artist was outlandish; she wanted to learn more about him.

She started feeling uncomfortable due to her menstrual cycle. She always wondered if menstruation was a curse or a boon for girls in a country such as India. She hated the impure status given to women during their period by fanatics. But these straying thoughts didn't deter her from her objective of searching for information about the artist who was alien to her. She googled the internet and found nothing about the uncelebrated artist. Every attempt went in vain. Porn site pop up ads maddened her and she felt like thrashing her laptop. After hours of disappointment, she found a Facebook link which led to the artist's profile.

There was a surprise waiting for her. It was a *wow* moment for her. The anonymous artist was an Alma Mater of the university from where she would be graduating. She didn't know how to get more information about the artist. Days rolled on; she gathered the courage to send a Facebook friend request and the request was accepted. The moment she saw the request being accepted she felt like painting the town red.

She became addicted to stalking. It became a daily ritual for her. She indulged in it religiously. She started trailing him to erase a picture from her heart. She knew each and every post about him on social networks. She could even recall the tagline verbatim with ease. Her laptop had a folder dedicated to the downloaded pictures of the artist's work posted in his profile. Her personal favourites were the charcoal paintings of the artist.

Somewhere during the end of 2017, on a busy day, as she walked through the long corridor of her college, she accidentally saw the artist there. She was exhilarated and her heart started thumping. For a second, she imprudently thought that the walkway had become the sanctum sanctorum. She never had the courage to introduce herself and initiate a conversation.

Days passed by. Two years later, the stalking still continued; the artist never knew that his profile was being stalked. Now, how do I conclude the story of this fictional aficionado?

Years ago, the artist did have an admirer who enthusiastically commented and appreciated his work. He was not even known as an artist then. All his novice works lay dead in his personal space. Some works even rested underneath his cot. There was no one to celebrate and appreciate the self-taught artist. Almost sixteen years later, he had an ardent fan who followed his works, applauded and celebrated them. After closely following him on Facebook for a considerable period, she wished him on his birthday and received a simple 'thank you' in response. She did not possess the guts to proceed with the conversation fearing that he would snub her. She was heartbroken at times, but she was hopeful that she would get a chance to talk to him in person and at least take a selfie with him some day.

Everything was like a lucid dream, like Sylvia Plath's quote, "I shut my eyes and all the world drops dead, I lift my eyes and all is born again." When she lifted her eyes, the world was new and strange to her. She had already befriended the artist. It was a Sunday morning; she was going to meet the artist for the first time. She was nervous and insecure; she felt that she was going to faint. She didn't know how to react and she had never felt this way before. Her heart fluttered. She could feel her blood gushing through her arteries. Her palms were sweating and tremorous. She had requested him to write a letter for her, which she would keep as a souvenir.

He was already waiting at the coffee shop for her; he was dressed in a black t-shirt which read 'Science, it works bitches!' and a faded pair of denim jeans. He wore a pair of glasses which transformed his look. She saw him reading a book by Frank Kafka. Kafka wasn't an unfamiliar name to her. Her grandmother had narrated the story of metamorphosis to her when she was in high school. For a second, she felt the artist to be Kafkaesque; she smiled to herself.

She said, "Hi, Sir."

"Hey, hello...how are you?" asked the artist with a congenial smile. "What would you like to have?" he asked.

"Anything, Sir, it's your choice," she replied.

A hot cup of cappuccino was served on the table. Though she preferred espresso shots she didn't mind. The aroma of the roasted coffee beans filled the air-conditioned coffee house. Phil Collin's *Another Day in Paradise* was playing in the background. Their conversation continued. They spoke about art, science, books and common interests. An hour had already passed by and she felt she was in a state of suspended animation. She expected him to give her the letter she had requested. She wasn't comfortable asking for it, but her heart really begged for him to give her the letter.

His mobile rang; his ringtone was an old classical song. She expected something better. He spoke to someone, his loud voice disrupting the ambience. She admired his care-a-damn attitude and she wished he could be her mentor.

"Okay then, nice meeting you, we'll catch up sometime later," he told her.

She was about to collapse as she was yet to get the letter. There was a pause. She felt she was on the verge of crying. She felt he was cantankerous and she cursed him. He walked out of the coffee shop without looking back. She sat still for a while, her expectations shattered. Suddenly, she saw him striding towards her. "I'm sorry," he said, in a persuasive tone, "I forgot to give this to you." He retrieved a handmade paper folded like origami from the book he was carrying. Oops! He must be an Akira Yoshizawa admirer, she felt. She caressed the texture of the handmade paper. She did not know what was written inside. She desperately wanted his autograph but she now possessed a letter exclusively written for her.

The letter read as follows:

I have been empty-headed, not knowing that someone has been stalking me incognito. When you revealed to me that it was you, I became inarticulate. It was an animated silence.

After days of sugar-coated conversations, you asked me to pen down a personal letter to you in an old-fashioned style that you admire. To be truthful, my paraphernalia refuses to move. I'm devoid of words that will galvanize your thoughts.

This letter will most certainly be plain vanilla amidst the modern-day pandemonium of digital conversation. It may lack connotations and witticisms. It may not be nearly as visually appealing as Van Gogh's The Starry Night or as compelling as Shakespeare's Macbeth. It may lack metaphors; it may not be bombastic.

I just want to make it simple. Life is just a cosmic blink; and for me more than a decade was lost in ho-hum and humdrum events.

I struggle to conclude. I'm unsure how to sign off. I would rather end with an ellipsis instead of a full stop...

Below is one line to summarize my thoughts:

"You came as a petrichor on a desert to celebrate my creativity."

As usual, this line sounded cryptic to her like his painting. Before she could finish reading his letter, he vanished into the crowd. She wished to see him one more time. Kafka's quote came to her mind: I miss you deeply, unfathomably, senselessly, terribly.

A Scorpio Cuckolded...

She was nearing her forty-second birthday. She was unaware of how time had flown by. It had been twenty years since she had tied the knot. All her time had been spent nurturing her children. She had never dreamt of entertainment in any form. She was married to her maternal uncle whom she loved; time rolled on without any memorable occasions. Off late, she began to show signs of irritation. Very often, to her co-workers, she felt drained and worn-out. She felt like a beautiful bird flapping it wings inside a golden cage.

Her body showed signs of early menopause. Her husband was a bigot and chauvinist. He was strict and a man of his own principles. He worked for a private firm and he was married to his work. The only entertainment he opted for was sex with his helpless wife. Sex was a boring routine for her. It was like one more household chore. She never knew what an orgasm felt like. She was a typical Indian wife who had never dared fantasize about other men in bed.

A few days after her forty-second birthday, her father was diagnosed with carcinoma of the lungs. It came as a big shock to her since her father was a teetotaller and a fitness buff. Months elapsed with oncologist's visits, radiotherapy and chemotherapy, et cetera. Her father counted down his days and was eventually hospitalized with a terminal illness. She spent her nights in the waiting room as an attendant for her father who was admitted to the intensive care unit. Nothing seemed more important to her than her ailing father.

She knew every other patient's attendant who waited along with her. She sensed despair in every attendant's face, waiting for the intercom in the room to ring. The moment the intercom rang, every attendant's heartrate would rise in unison until the patient's bed number was announced. Her father's bed number was 26 in the ICU. On and off the central paging system would announce some doctor's name. Sometimes, when she heard a code blue page, she hoped it wouldn't be bed number 26. She carried Paul Kalanithi's *When Breath Becomes Air* to keep herself awake at night. But she was unaware that it was the wrong book to be reading at this miserable phase in her life. Her mind was in a pathetic state, feeling nothingness. Midlife crisis had taken its toll, with physical ailments showing early signs of mortality.

A major part of her life had elapsed in an androcentric social circle. Her world revolved around the wellbeing of others; she never had time to breath for herself. This is a common state of most middle-class women in Indian families.

The attendant for bed number 26 was summoned immediately at 1:00 a.m. The walkway of the hospital was deserted. The midnight was buried in grave silence. The elevator was in auto mode. The lift operator was in deep sleep, snoring loudly. *Do not enter; remove your footwear*, the door sign said. She used a shoe cover from an automatic dispenser and entered the ICU.

The intensivist briefed her about her father's health; a tracheotomy was necessary to save her sinking father. He required artificial ventilation. Tears rolled down her face. She was requested to sign a consent form. She remembered her childhood days when she would wait with anxiety to get her progress card signed by her father. Today, she had to sign a form for him. Her heart galloped when she signed the consent form. The beeping noise from the monitors in the ICU made her mad. She wished such moments would vanish like magic.

Close to ten days had passed in the hospital; everyone in the family was losing their patience and faith. They were prepared for any outcome. That night, it was raining. It was the southwest summer monsoon. It was her turn to stay the night in the waiting room. She had already lost a few pounds and had developed dark circles around her eyes due to lack of sleep. The book she was carrying had not been read.

She looked at her mobile and it suddenly vibrated. She found that she had been added to some WhatsApp group titled *Nostalgic Memories*. She wasn't keen on knowing more about it. Just as she was about to leave the group, she noticed that it was her old college mates. She browsed through the members of the group. She did not have most of their contact numbers. She tried to peg her old classmates from their display photographs. Most of them had changed. She could see grey hairs and wrinkles on most of their faces which made it difficult to recognize them. Her eyes eagerly scrutinized for someone special in the group. She found him. The moment she saw his photograph her adrenaline levels shot up. An unfathomable emotion welled up within her.

Her memory registered his mobile number. She wanted to call him immediately. Her fingers acted reflexively but the hospital clock struck twelve. She thought it wouldn't be right to call him at this time. Her thoughts were disturbed. Momentarily, her thoughts were removed from the deteriorating health of her father. She stared blankly at her mobile when suddenly it vibrated briefly. Even the vibrating mobile made an audible noise in the waiting room. She received a personal message from the most unexpected person; it was from the number she had just noted down. She felt her nerves go through a brief electric shock.

"Hi, how are you," the text read.

She didn't know how to respond. He surely must have noticed the double blue tick marks at the end of his message.

"Hey, are you there?" read another message. A thin film of tears covered her eyes, but she did not want to cry in front of others, revealing her fragility. She picked up her mobile and walked to the cafeteria. She ordered a cup of coffee; a steaming hot cup of coffee was like fomentation therapy for her momentarily.

She had the audacity to reply to the number after hesitating for a few minutes. He must have been waiting for her message. He replied immediately. They slowly started exchanging text messages, asking each other formal questions. They chatted for quite some time now. Both of them hesitated to talk to each other. There were certain things that were best communicated through text they felt.

He broke the silence. He asked if he could call her. "Not now," she said instantaneously. She was not prepared to hear his voice which she had admired once. He must have felt bad.

"Okay then, I will text you tomorrow. Take care," he responded.

It sounded abrupt, she thought. "Okay, bye," was all she could manage. She knew he was upset but she was not in a state to talk to him.

The next few days were traumatic. Her father's status fluctuated. Her mobile remained dead without charge over these days. This didn't even bother her. She had to stay the night at the hospital the following weekend. She switched on her mobile. She was flooded with a barrage of messages. There were useless forwards, umpteen good morning messages, some memes trolling politicians, some hate messages, et cetera. She scanned for a special message from a hotchpotch of unwanted texts. "Voila!" she said, on seeing his message.

He was younger than her by two years. They had been close friends in college. He was in love with her and had proposed to her once. She had declined his proposal for pragmatic reasons. He pretended to accept her decision and continued to be her friend till their farewell. Today, after twenty years, he was a successful businessman. She thought his wife must be very lucky. But destiny had a different story to write. Their marriage had been fractured from the very first day. The biggest mistake of his life was being honest about his past with his fiancé during their courtship.

It was 9:30 p.m. She went to the ICU. Her father's condition was status quo. She walked on the ramp. She saw a huge idol of Mother Mary. Though she was a Hindu by birth, she stood there for a while and offered her prayers. She hoped for a miracle to happen. She sat for a while, debating whether she should call him or not. Eventually, she gathered her confidence to call him. Her heart beat like that of an adolescent. She had no clue what to say to him.

"Hello," she said.

"Just a second," came the reply. She had a faint memory of their conversations during their college days. "I'm sorry, my wife's about to doze off. I don't want to disturb her," he continued.

"Oh, sorry, shall I call you some other time?" she asked.

"Oh no, that's okay," he said. "Tell me, How are you?"

His words soothed her. She spoke for thirty minutes. She felt comfortable that he listened to her. She just needed a shoulder to lean on. She was exhausted and tired of her daily routine.

He said he would pay a visit to see her father in the hospital. "Please come before 7:30 p.m. Visiting hours are between 4:00 and 7:30 p.m." She hung up.

The following night, her father's health was stable, without many fluctuations. She longed for him and waited for visiting hours. They would be meeting each other after a long time. She felt some kind of inexplicable discomfort in anticipation of his visit. The clock ticked on. It was 7:30 p.m. Her expectations had gone in vain. She felt it was too much to expect him to visit. She knew expectations are the mother of disappointment. It was 8:00 p.m. She waited in the pharmacy for her token number to be displayed on the monitor to receive the drugs ordered for her father.

She felt lousy and sleepy. She was not able to stay awake. She took a quick nap when she heard someone call her by name. It was like a dream to her. She saw him standing right in front of her. He was well dressed. His opulence was visible in the way he carried himself. He was clean-shaven. She couldn't find a single grey hair on his head. She thought she looked old in front of him. He carried the latest iPhone. His mobile rang continuously. He must be a busy man, she thought.

"How are you," he asked.

"I'm okay."

"How is your father?"

Before she could answer him, someone interrupted. He was the chairman of the hospital. He had come to receive him. She wondered how influential he had grown in twenty years. He used to be kind of a nitwit in college. He spoke about the health status of her father and told her to call him directly should the need arise. The chairman shared his number with her and took leave.

They sat in the main lobby of the hospital. It was almost 8:30 p.m. They recalled nostalgic memories of their college days. The central paging system made announcements now and then. The hospital staff changed shifts. Diet trolleys moved in different directions. Her husband called her a few times. She did not know why she avoided telling him that she was with her old college friend.

They walked to the cafeteria. She ordered two coffees. He interrupted. "Sorry, don't you know I don't drink coffee?" he asked.

"I'm sorry, I forgot," she pretended. She knew that he didn't drink coffee but it was kind of a quick test for him to see whether he had changed. She took her handbag to pay the bill but he shoved her hands signalling that he would take care of it.

He said he would take leave but she wanted to spend more time with him. She said she would accompany him to the parking lot. He had driven to the hospital himself. He owned a luxury car with a fancy number plate. Both of them wanted time to freeze. His mobile screamed; this time, the ringtone was a distinct Tamil classical song. He spoke in a persuasive voice. "It's my wife," he said.

"Oh, okay. Sorry, I forgot to ask, how many children?"

"No, we are trying IVF," he said.

She was puzzled but kept silent. He got into his car, sat down and lowered his window. The car perfume surrounded the space around her. She was able to hear some old Tamil songs inside the car. He lowered the volume. "Then..." he said. It sounded ambiguous to her. He rested his elbow on the window, his diamond-studded gold ring glittering. It started to drizzle.

"I think it will rain. I will take leave," she said. Her emotions exploded. Her thoughts became unmanageable. She held his elbow tight, squashing it between her palm and finger. He was able to feel her nails. This touch communicated a lot more than words ever could. It meant a lot to him. He glanced up at her with misty eyes. Her eyes seemed regretful. She missed him. She wanted him back in her life. She wasn't ashamed of this thought though she was married. She remembered Osho quoting that marriage was immoral.

For moments, they only heard the wind rustling through the leaves of trees. Suddenly, the power went off and the generator was turned on. It disturbed the mood. He felt it was time to part. "Will you come again," she asked sceptically.

"Let me see, I'm not sure," he said.

The next morning, when she reached home, her husband forced himself on her. It was marital rape. She was helpless and reluctant, but this time it was a new experience for her. She did not know why she fantasized about her ex-boyfriend. She was on the brink of reaching her climax, but her husband's four-minute threshold was over. She wanted to attack him with all kinds of profanities she knew.

The following day, it was her husband's turn to stay at the hospital. She wished for an opportunity to do hospital duty. However, she did not want to volunteer and give him unnecessary clues. She feared that she would become an adulteress, but she also knew that nothing was unfair in love and war.

She expected him to call anytime. She hankered for his call. But she was also doubtful. With much hesitation, she called him once. "Hello, who is this? I'm in a meeting," he said in an authoritative tone. She felt disdain. All her excitement disappeared like a mirage; her transitory elephantine exhilaration was back to square one.

Her father's health yo-yoed up and down without much improvement. It was around 2:00 p.m., when she was taking her siesta, that a WhatsApp text disturbed her sleep.

"Hi, how are you?" the message said. It made her alert. She was infuriated since he had rebuffed her call. She wanted to cold-shoulder him; she did not reply for a while.

"Hey, how are you? Are you there? Are you okay?"

She didn't want to behave like a frenetic wife so she responded that she was okay. Their chat prolonged for hours; she tried to use emoticons while chatting, which wasn't a piece of cake. He asked her whether she would be at the hospital that evening. She felt it was a subtle way to ask her on a date. "No, today it's my husband's turn. Would you like to come home? The children are at my mother's place. Nobody's around," she said. Without any second thoughts, he said no.

"Do you want to meet someplace else?" she asked.

"My office is near the crossroads," he suggested.

"No, no, not today. But I will surely come someday," she said, giving him cues.

They met in a south Indian restaurant. He sat in front of her and placed the order for her. She was surprised that he hadn't forgotten her favourite dish. She admired the way he ate; he had the same style of dining as her father. That night, her thoughts were preoccupied with memories of him. Not once did she think of her deteriorating father. She eagerly waited to see him again. Her long-lost passion was waiting to spread its wings like a forest fire.

The family had made up its mind to sign a 'do not resuscitate' order. The nurse in the ICU retrieved a red pen from her stained uniform pocket and marked the case file as DNR. Her father's face was bloated and the stink of faeces, urine and medicines permeated the air. The ventilator gushed air into his lungs. She was unable to see her father this way. She started crying. She knew that she had to cry silently without disturbing the other patients at the private hospital. Otherwise, she would be asked to leave. She was not able to bare the pain her father was going through. She wanted him to die peacefully; she wanted to sit beside him and hold his hand tight when he passed on.

A text message disrupted her pain. "I'm waiting in the parking area," said the message. She knew it was him. She asked her husband to stay near her father, telling him she would be back in a while. He didn't question where she was off to. He understood she was in miserable pain. It was late at night; she walked alone to the parking lot. She was in tears. The moment she saw his car she got into it. She burst out crying again. Suddenly, she turned towards him and hugged him tightly. He was able to feel her tears. He didn't know how to react. His arms hesitated to embrace her. A few minutes passed by. He was not able to resist her warmth. He had always longed for her hug, but he felt it had come at the wrong time. She didn't stop him. Her tears had stopped by then. He progressed to touch her. He felt jittery. He was able to feel her beautiful, sagging bosoms. He was not able to withdraw his hands. She felt her soul levitate. His mouth struggled to feel her tits. He could not resist leaving love bites on her bosom. He pulled her dress up and thrust his hand down. She fell flat, unable to resist him. Her G spot yearned for his touch. His fingers were wet and behaved as if he was dealing with a call girl. The moment she felt his fingers there, she felt all her neurons in her brain ignited. It was as if her brain cells were salsa dancing. For the first time in her life, she climaxed. Even before she could gather her composure, her husband called.

"Where are you," he asked?

She was jolted out of her euphoria. "I'm in the cafeteria," she said.

"I'm sorry, dear, your father has left us. The doctors declared him dead a few minutes ago. Please come soon," he said.

She remembered the passages from "My Father's Death and Double Shame" in Mahatma Gandhi's *The Story of My Experiments With Truth.*

The Crowned Demon and a Silent Angel

It was 2:00 a.m. on the 5th consecutive day of night duty during the second wave of Covid 19 in Chennai. Aadhi had penned a writeup and sent it to his buddy who always reviewed it before it was posted on any social media platform. It was a lengthy write up. He didn't know what had gone wrong. There was a ghostly disappearance of the write up. There was no room for pain and dismay over losses; everything seemed to be uncertain.

When your physical and mental state is completely worn out due to stress, there is a route to escape to the land of nowhere through your creativity, he thought. The second wave had created havoc. Every city in India was swept away in an infectious avalanche. The pandemonium created by ambulances speeding across cities in all directions made the heart skip a beat. The atmosphere was filled with a sense of fear and depression.

Round-the-clock, health professionals were on their toes. Every moment was challenging, every second was unprecedented. Every hospital had long queues of ambulances where patients waited to be attended to. What had gone wrong? Where were we heading to? What would be the state tomorrow? All these random questions haunted him. Was the sky falling down or was it a viral apocalypse?

Every loud cry in the silence of the night was in memory of someone whose life had been snatched by this micro monster. Inside every black body bag there lay a motionless person who had lost his or her battle against the virus. Every breath had been stolen by a biological malware. Some blamed it on gene splicing, some conspired it to be biological warfare, some said it was international political arm-wrestling, some hypothesized it to be a manipulation of the pharma industry. Whatever it was, there were zillions who had lost their lives.

Nature had once again proved that human knowledge was grossly insufficient. We had the technology to wipe out every life form on the face of this earth but we lacked the knowledge to save dying patients. The rattling of stretchers carrying dead bodies, the bovine cough, the cacophony of suffering patients, the tears, the grieving, the bone chilling drama, everything contributed to the increasing depression. The hissing of a ventilator, the bubbling of oxygen over the simple humidifier, the sight of a patient lying amidst the tubes and lines, the struggle to take a breath, the isolation from friends and relatives pierced Aadhi's heart with multiple arrows. He was an anaesthetist at a government hospital. His job magnificently mutilated him.

Lack of sufficient medical oxygen, lack of sufficient hospital beds, lack of remedies... everything was beyond his control. Death was in the air. Everyone prayed for their safety and that of their dear ones. During all this chaos, Aadhi sat meditating in the doctor's room. He tried to divert his thoughts through mindful meditation. But he wasn't able to focus. His focus was distracted by memories of his ex-girlfriend Subha, whom he had seen after eight years in the hospital he worked. She had meant a lot to him. He never expected to meet her again in his life. It had been four days since her husband had admitted her in the government hospital.

Aadhi wore a PPE and his identity was not visible. He saw her sitting on the pavement. He was unable to accept what he saw. "How are you?" he wanted to ask her, but he refrained from doing so. His spectacles were fogged. His faceguard prevented him from being recognized. She was sick. He remembered her beautiful smile. Now, wrinkles on her forehead betrayed her hardships.

She was RT PCR positive; he did not understand what she was going through. The outpatient, zero-delay, fever clinic was flooded with sick, helpless patients. It was already 9:00 p.m. The gloomy night, the odour of the hospital, the rasping sound of coughs everywhere and the long queue of ambulances created panic. The resident doctor in the clinic checked her oxygen saturation. The pulse oximeter, after some hesitation, revealed a reading of 93 mm hg, and her heart rate was 85.

The physician requested an ECG and a complete blood count. There was only one wheelchair; its wheels creaked, making a loud noise. He managed to move her to the ECG room. There was an obese Muslim lady coughing loudly underneath her burka. He wondered if she was wearing a mask. The ECG technician was a gorgeous, beautiful girl. She wore a skin-hugging white top through which her nipples protruded. Every time she leaned forward, her dusky, soft breasts peeped out of her V neck collar. Her eyes were black and they had thousand stories to narrate. He had no interest in ogling at her. The technician shouted in her loud voice to organise the crowds waiting for an ECG.

Subha was fragile and weak. She was unable to climb on to the couch to have her ECG recording done. The technician managed to record it as she sat in her wheel chair. She pulled out the ECG graph and handed it over to Aadhi. He was apprehensive about reading the ECG report given the knowledge he possessed. The next step was blood extraction, to do the complete blood count. The phlebotomists were busy. It was their dinner time. The whole hospital was busy. There was an outdoor broadcast unit waiting outside the hospital. Journalists were doing their media coverage. There was live relay of breaking news about the Covid situation around the country.

He received a phone call from one of his friends enquiring about the availability of the drug Remdesivir. The in-charge physician screamed to have the crowds cleared. After much struggle and formalities, she was admitted in the G wing of the second floor Corona block. The liftman was energetic. He did not wear his mask properly. His height must have been only 145 cm which would qualify him to be labelled a dwarf in India.

The elevator door opened and there was a stretcher which entered with a black body bag. I just observed the transparent part of the body bag that revealed the deceased man's face. He must have been in his twenties; his face wore a beard which hadn't been shaved for a few days. A housekeeping staff squeezed herself into the lift.

After hours of struggle, they got a bed with oxygen support for her. Her husband was not allowed inside the Corona wards. Before leaving, he spoke some reassuring words to his wife. No visitor was allowed to see Covid patients to avoid cross-infection. Her eyes were blank. She was unable to comprehend what was happening around her.

On the first day, she managed the stress of her sickness and the hospital which resembled a Auschwitz concentration camp. No one was sure if they would return home alive. For those who made it, the meaning of life made sense.

The following day, her condition worsened, but no information was given to her relatives; Aadhi did not know her husband's number. She had a mobile phone but accidently, it fell from her bed and shattered into pieces. The contact number given in her admission records was incorrect. It was illegible. He didn't know what to do. He rushed to the attender's waiting area to check if he could find her husband whose face he vaguely remembered. He was not able to identify him.

He decided to stay with her. The PPE was useful to hide his identity. He did everything for her. She was not even able to walk to the restroom. He helped her with the bedpan and put the adult diapers for her.

Subha never knew who was helping her. She thought that her husband had arranged for a male caretaker for her. She addressed him as brother in her feeble voice if she needed something. Her sugar levels had gone up drastically; she was slowly deteriorating. She wanted to see her husband and her child. Aadhi requested for permission from the floor-in-charge. They denied his request owing to hospital protocol. He consoled her and said that they would come during visiting hours.

Often, there would be a death in the ward. One after the other, people were dying. The panic created by the frequent deaths killed every inmate slowly. Subha was slowly losing the battle; her lips were dry and her skin, peeling. Her gums bled for unknown reasons. Her oxygen saturation slowly dipped; she required ventilator support, but there were no beds available in the Intensive Care Unit.

She continued to deteriorate. He was able to feel the darkness of death invade her. Aadhi went begging for an ICU bed. The ICU was flooded and looked like a gateway to nowhere. Every other bed had a dead body which was shifted to the morgue. The fifty-body capacity morgue was packed with nearly three hundred bodies. The bodies lay piled up like on a battlefield.

Only when someone died the bed would become vacant for a patient in the ward to move to. Time was running out. The chance of getting a bed in the ICU was minimal. He prayed for a miracle to happen, but his rational self knew that miracles were foreordained. Whatever happened, happened the way it was destined to happen. He started sweating profusely inside the PPE. He could feel his latex gloves fill with sweat quickly. He was unable accept her deteriorating health. He felt like his heart was crumbling. He heard her feeble voice calling out to her child.

When you realise you are going to die, you need someone you love beside you, to hold your hand and say a warm goodbye to a world of annihilation. Her oxygen saturation receded rapidly. Her pulse decreased too. He did not know what to do. None of her relatives were around. This was during the period the whole hospital was contagious. At any time, anyone would pick up an infection if they were careless about their safety protocols.

He couldn't bear to witness her death. He decided to take off his PPE and hold her hand, give her the comfort of a known face when she departed. He removed his PPE, held her hand and said, "Subha, I'm here with you, don't be afraid, you are all right." Her drained, fading memories tapering into oblivion had no time to be startled by the sight of him. Her pupils moved once and became motionless and benumbed, those eyes directly gazing into his, never blinking again. He looked into her eyes. He saw his reflection in her immobile eyes. Adhi"s tears poured on to her frozen eyes and rolled down her dead face. It looked like a visual metaphor, as though she was crying for him.

He knew he would never overcome the pain of her death, but his rational mind understood that nothingness was the essence of life. Her hands still held him; he felt the last warmth of her body. There was a calendar on the wall making squeaky sounds as it moved in the fresh breeze coming in through the window. The bright green letters printed on the broken white background stated: "And their hands will speak to us." – Al-Qur'an

Andaman, Jarawa and a
Strange Love Story

It was August, 2018; it was when he was going though tremendous stress due to the court hearing and his failure to pass the competitive exam to enter government service. He needed a break to relax and recuperate.

He decided to travel alone to Andaman and Nicobar Islands. He never knew why he decided to visit these islands. The day he reached Port Blair, he visited some beaches and Kaala Paani jail. He was a photography enthusiast; a mirrorless camera was new gear to him. He was trying to figure out the possibilities in his new camera. Whatever the art form, the outcome is more astounding when the creator is depressed. He had always wondered if there was a connection between art and stress. It was as though you dip the brush in the paint which is a cocktail of stress hormones.

The day was a bit ho-hum; the weather was fickle and unpredictable. It was a dry day and he was unable to identify a watering hole. He was desperate for a drink. He managed to get a bottle of Smirnoff vodka. He gulped four large shots and was quickly inebriated. He got lost and ended up hanging out in weird places with some odd characters. Somehow, he found an auto-rickshaw driver who knew where Circuit House was in Port Bair.

The next day, he planned to visit the limestone caves and sand volcanos. The caves were more than a hundred kilometres away, on Baratang Island.

He got up at 2:30 a.m. and started his journey by 3:00 a.m. in a private tourist car. The driver was a young guy. He spoke fluent Hindi and chewed *paan* constantly. By 4:56 a.m. the sun was set to rise. It happened much earlier than in south India. He reached the convoy check-post by 5:00 a.m. There were many cars already waiting there and more cars and buses joined later. An announcement was made through the public address system. It announced the dos and don'ts of the convoy through Andaman Trunk Road.

The check post had a few tea and coffee shops; he walked into one. It started raining. The rain made loud noises as it slashed against the rusted and corroded metal roof of the small eatery where he sat. The intensity of the rain decreased and it started to drizzle. As he listened to the soft and continuous raindrops as they hit the roof, all his memories came back to him. But they were not discrete and separate from each other. Instead, all of his memories seemed to have formed a patchwork, becoming entwined with one another.

He had to submit some government identity proof to pass through the reserve forest. Cars weren't permitted to stop along the fifty-kilometre drive as it passed through the restricted Jarawa reserve tribal belt. Amidst this hustle and bustle, he found a young girl all alone; she looked anxious and confused. She seemed to be late and was trying to find a specific vehicle in the convoy. He was least interested in what happened to her. He sat in his car and waited for the convoy to start. Suddenly, he saw her running toward his car and plead with his driver in Hindi. She requested a hitchhike. The driver dismissed her request. As the car started moving, he asked the driver to allow her to accompany them.

She thanked him a lot and sat next to the driver. It was sharp 6:30 a.m. when the convoy started moving at a slow pace; thirty to forty kilometres was the speed limit. It was as though we were entering into a paradise of pitch silence. The reserve forest was inhabited by the Jarawa tribe. Most people came here to sightsee the

Jarawa tribals. It was marketed like a human zoo.

All that was heard in the silence was the sound of motor engines and birds chirping. Her headphones were so loud that he was able hear the song she was listening to; it was an old Latha Mangeshkar song. Though the sound bothered him, he was in no mood to pay any attention to it. She turned towards him and tried to start a conversation; he never responded. He was drenched in thoughts of the past. He even lacked social etiquette. She was the exact opposite of him, full of zest for life. She enjoyed every moment. He was able to see her through the rear-view mirror.

All of a sudden, her zest vanished and was invaded by glimpses of pain; her mood fluctuated like the Andaman weather. She was beautiful; her straightened, soft, black hair with streaks of burgundy added to her beauty. She was very attractive. He saw her eyes; they were almond-shaped and looked fabulous. Her left eye deviated slightly but even this added to her beauty. Occasionally, she looked down at her black, full sleeves t-shirt. It was as though she glanced at her femininity with pride. She had a small pimple on her fore head. She was seemingly beautiful.

After a long, bumpy ride, they reached Baratang. He eagerly waited to visit the limestone caves. To his dismay, there was a strike by the locals in operating the speed boats. He had to visit the sand volcanoes which were nearby. She accompanied him. They saw some Jarawas in the nearby rehabilitation camp. He started clicking photos of the blue sea and some rusted ferries. He waited for a chance to click her portrait candidly without her knowledge. Her beauty was so mesmerising and irresistible that anyone would be compelled to befriend her.

Slowly, she started conversing with him on the ferry ride. She felt he was hard to crack. Over time, he started responding slowly. After talking to her for a bit, he came to know she was a post graduate in psychology. Her name was Erina. It sounded like a Muslim name but she wasn't wearing a burkha. Their conversation continued. She was from Kolkata. She confirmed that she was a Muslim and that it was suffocating underneath the burkha. She was engaged to be married in a couple of months. She wasn't inclined towards the match and wanted to break free. She wanted to flap her wings and fly free.

It was already 6:00 p.m. when they reached Port Blair. The ferry ride was nauseating and she was close to being seasick. Her mobile phone alerted her of a message. It was from her airlines company. Her flight had been postponed due to bad weather. She had no plans to spend the night at Port Blair. She did not know what to do and could not afford a hotel room. He asked her what the problem was? He said she could stay in his room if she felt he was trust worthy. She had always liked taking risks. She pretended to decline his offer. After a bit of persuasion, she accepted.

It was almost 10:00 p.m. when they reached the room. He asked her to make herself comfortable. The room was cluttered. Half a bottle of vodka lay on the table with junk food and peanuts around it. She washed her face and tied her hair up. She sat on the bed and began flipping through TV channels. He asked her if she drank. She said no. "Can I see the snaps you clicked today?" she asked. He was a bit hesitant since he had discreetly taken a picture of her. He handed his camera over to her. "If you want, you can have a drink, I don't mind," she said.

Time elapsed. There was some music channel playing continuously in the back ground. She saw her portrait in the camera but didn't react. She felt no one else could have shot her better. She admired herself in the picture, zooming in and out. He bowed his head down as though he had committed a crime. "When did you click this? It's superb!" she said. His feel-good hormones were boosted.

"Have you ever tasted alcohol," he asked.

"Yep, once, it was a Breezer. Later, I did not find a reliable crime partner to share a drink."

"Do you want try now?"

She hesitated. "Do you want me to?" she asked.

"Why not? Give it a try," he said. He mixed the drink meticulously like a bartender.

She was slightly intoxicated and began sharing pleasantries. All of a sudden, she turned toward him and asked, "Can I kiss you?" He was shocked and blunt. He asked her why, even though he wanted to be physical with her. She said she had always fantasized about having sex with a stranger. He felt as though it was a blank cheque. "If you feel this way, we can..." he said.

She pulled his head towards her and they smooched mouth to mouth. It was an extended, long kiss. He had never ever experienced such a kiss. She threw herself on the bed and pulled her black t-shirt up. Her bosom was full; it seemed to suffocate inside her black bra. She extended her arms and invited him to come on top of her. His left hand made its way behind her back and unbuckled her straps. He felt dizzy. Her bosoms were firm. When he came over her, drops of his sweat fell on her bosoms. They shattered and disappeared in her firmness.

Her body odour was strong. He dipped his face into her axilla. His tongue wandered the surface of her bosom and started guzzling her teats. "Should I really go any further," he asked.

"Don't talk, just do it," she responded.

He removed her jeans and greedily entered her, breaking her virginity. She started bleeding.

"I'm sorry," he said.

"Don't be," she responded.

It was a memorable night for him. He never knew when he had dozed off. After several years, he had slept peacefully.

The following day, he woke up at around 8:00 a.m. He felt a bit sluggish. The doors were open. He was not able to find Erina. She had disappeared. It was as if he had had a pleasant dream. His heart ached, but it was of no use.

A year passed by. He was waiting at the airport to board a flight. He saw a Muslim woman sitting opposite him. Her eyes seemed very familiar. He gathered all his courage to talk to her. The moment he stood up, there was an announcement that his flight was ready to board. He didn't want to miss this chance. He went close to her. Just then, he heard a male voice saying, "Erina, let's move," in Urdu. He stood still.

Nothing makes a room feel emptier than wanting someone in it.

The whiskey whispered...

It was nine past five in the middle of summer 2020. As usual, he was reading a book authored by Kamala Das, a female cult writer in Malayalam. There was a message notification from an unknown number. Five minutes passed by. He was least bothered to know who had sent him the text. Lately, there was no one who dedicated their time to talk or chat with an old, rotting rat like him. He assumed that it was a natural death for many intelligent people.

He put a morsel of *dosa* into his mouth while his left hand quickly scanned his text messages. One message read as follows: "Hi, Sir. This is Aarathi." The double "A" was an unusual way of writing this name. He thought it could probably have some numerological significance. The message continued. "At present, I'm posted as an intern in an IT firm and I specialize in AI. I have certain doubts related to my career and I would like to discuss them with you. I would like to see you in person and get some clarity on them. I hardly have two days left to complete my internship after which I will be leaving for my native. What would be the right time to meet you, Sir?"

He read her message carefully. "Hi," he replied. Next, he checked out her display photograph. She hadn't posted it. He usually had two opinions about people who hid their identity. It was either lack of confidence about their looks or the fear of someone downloading their photograph. He was not really in a mood to judge her personality. He promised to meet her at his work place. He had no expectations regarding this meeting. He didn't know what was in his kitty.

The next day, he was busy organizing things for a client meeting. There were too many trainees in his firm. Everyone wore a face mask to protect themselves from the corona virus infection. With the mask, everyone looked beautiful. He thought that the brain was hardwired to perceive every face to be beautiful. Most often, perception is not the reality. He had been disappointed with the distortion of his perception on seeing some faces which he had perceived to be the most beautiful.

It was very hot because of the early summer. His firm was on the eighth floor and sea-facing. He always relaxed on seeing the sea and the busy harbour in the distance. That day, the local electricity board had a maintenance power shutdown. He sweated a lot. He tried to get some cool breeze, standing near a window, hoping that the cool breeze would stop him from sweating. He turned around to witness a gust in a yellow outfit. He never knew who she was. She was well-groomed and knew how to carry herself. Her black eyes sparkled above her crimson face mask. It was a kind of weapon she possessed with which she could pulverize any man's heart. She had a folder on her fore arm and her dupatta modestly covered one side of her bosom. She looked like a celluloid heroine for a moment.

She walked towards him. Until that instant, he had never known who she was. "What do you want?" he asked rudely.

"Sir, it was me who had messaged you last evening," came a nuanced voice. He expected an unconventional looking person, but she was a conservative woman. His mind hypothetically characterized her personality. As he wanted her to feel comfortable, he gestured to her to take a seat. Her eyes stole the show. He didn't know whether her heartbeat was racing, but it would be no surprise if his heart skipped a beat. The missing spaces would be filled with her beautiful image.

She sat down and bowed and looked into her feminine pride. He was not able to figure out this cryptic gesture. He sat in front of her and she lowered her face mask. His eyes popped out of his head with astonishment when he saw her innocent, unadulterated beauty. He cursed himself for not being a portrait photographer. He wanted to freeze this moment and preserve it.

She was not articulate to start with. Even he fumbled when he tried to start a conversation with her. "Tell me, then?" he said. He guessed she had rehearsed what she was going to say to him. She spoke about her career and future plans. He was naive in answering her queries, but he did give her suggestions with his limited knowledge. That day was just like a miracle.

A few days passed by. She had started chatting with him whenever time permitted. Initially, he was unable to comprehend her complex personality. He couldn't figure out if she was an aficionado or a friend. She used to send him lengthy mails, sharing with him all the good things that had happened in her life. She invited him to come to her native, Kolkata.

One dull Sunday afternoon, she was chatting with him and out of the blue the conversation turned steamy. He didn't have time to comprehend what had really happened. Things got out of control. Her message read, "I feel wet on my vulva." He was equally wet. He begged her to call him on his phone. But she declined. She told him it was better this way. The texting continued for a while and suddenly there was silence on both ends. The silence loudly moaned in his head. Both of them had experienced biological orgasms through a virtual medium.

There were multiple orgasms on multiple occasions through phone sex. They both cleanly had a dirty relationship, third wheeled by a 4G network. Almost two years had passed by since he had first met her. For reasons not well understood, he lost contact with her. She seldom invaded him in his dreams. His heart longed to chat and share some good moments with her. It was the sixth wave of the covid pandemic. Though things were under control, people were forced to stay inside their homes due to the strict lockdown.

It was late at night; he was watching an old Malayalam film called *Kumbalani Nights*. His whisky glass was half full. He often became weirdly courageous when he was drunk. He started searching for her name on Facebook. After hours of struggle, he found her. Her profile stated that she lived in New York. He gained the courage to message her on Facebook. For a while, there was no response. All of a sudden, he saw her typing the reply. He eagerly waited to chat with her. His heart was thumping. He was unable to comprehend his emotions. He didn't understand why tears rolled down his cheeks. It was a kind of tricky feeling. He began to feel as though he was going to have a panic attack.

The reply came.

"Hi, this is Aarathi's husband. She's not interested in talking to you anymore and it would be appreciated if you don't attempt to get in touch with her hereafter."

For a moment, he felt his brain was sucked into a vacuum bubble. He felt like he had Cotard Syndrome. Tears rolled down his cheeks. What else could a helpless emotion do? He poured two large neats and chugged them.

Dreelissa

It was November 2016. They were the last few days she was going to spend in Chennai. She was going to be separated from her love by a distance of five hundred kilometres. Though she could stay in touch with him virtually, the thought of physical separation was very painful. Vivian was his name; it was an unusual name for a south Indian. It probably came about because of his father's interest in linguistics.

She had already booked her bus ticket to return to her native. They had both decided to spend quality time together. They didn't understand Hindi but they watched a Hindi film named *Ae Dill Hai Mushkil.* Hardly anybody was there in the theatre. The corner seats encouraged romance. He clasped her hands; her tender palms started sweating. He had always witnessed her palms sweat during an emotional drive. Suddenly, the theatre audio system started screaming the song *Bulleya.* As the music reached its crescendo, she wasn't able to control herself. She pulled him towards her and kissed him intensely. By the time they could go any further, the song had come to an end. The film got over at 3:00 p.m. They headed towards their hostel in a two-wheeler. She hated that he did not wear his helmet. She refused to ride pillion with him if he didn't wear his helmet. The helmet was her birthday gift to him. Halfway through the ride, they stopped near a *paani poori* street food shop. She could eat paani poori any time of day or night. The way she effortlessly ate the *paani poori* without spilling needs some expertise, he thought.

Two days later, she would leave for her hometown. She wanted to visit the museum in Chennai. She had recently changed her deodorant and its fragrance registered in her memories. That day, she wore a nice white t-shirt and denim jeans. The t-shirt had 'Rock my Life' printed on it.

Their tour of the museum was engaging. She admired his knowledge in archaeology and his interest in palaeontology. It was rare that an engineering student would be interested in this subject, she thought. Somehow, it was this characteristic that had attracted her to him in the first place. He had Rs 700 left in his purse. This was the last of the money which he had taken from his parents. Both of them had been selected during the campus interviews and their placement was due in December. He filled petrol for two hundred rupees. On the way back, she leaned against him. He was able to feel the warmth of her love. She brought her thighs together but she found he had no reaction. He must be a dumb ass, she thought. He was not able to get her cues. She decided not to give any cryptic clues; it was better to be straightforward. That afternoon had been heavenly for her. She felt as though a thousand rockets had been ignited for launch. It was like a biological cosmic collision.

After hours of crying, they parted with pain. He saw her off at the Chennai Mofussil Bus Terminus. He wondered if somebody had deliberately coined the word Mofussil which is derived from the Arabic word 'Mufaṣṣal' meaning to be separated. In a few moments, they would be separated. It was 10:00 p.m. on November 8. The bus moved slowly out of the terminus. Her eyes were filled with tears. He felt it was doomsday. The pain was insufferable. He stood alone until the bus disappeared in the city traffic.

Her face flashed in his thoughts every second. She called him around 1:00 a.m. She was sobbing as she said she missed him acutely. He was sleepless throughout that night. He decided to meet her on her birthday which was on November 13, and surprise her. It was the last day at the hostel. Every student had vacated the hostel. He decided to meet her on her birthday and then go to his native.

Four days flew by like seconds. He didn't leave the hostel and eagerly waited to meet her. On Saturday, he went to the bus terminus to take a bus to her native. He hadn't reserved the ticket. He had his last Rs 500 left in his wallet. This note was not valid due to demonetization. He was hungry but unable to buy food with the demonetized money. He was not able to buy a bus ticket. He desperately wanted to surprise his girlfriend on her birthday. He decided to bike ride the five hundred kilometres. He filled petrol using his debit card.

She pinged him to say hi. "Advance birthday wishes to my angelic soul," he responded. The conversation continued for a while. "Will you be awake at midnight?" he asked.

"I will wait for your first wish," she said.

He never revealed to her that he would be coming to meet her. He signed off saying, "Good night baby."

It was almost 10:00 p.m. He started his ride. It was cool breezy weather. The Doppler Effect produced by passing vehicles was mesmerizing. He plugged his earphones. His playlist was full of Rehman songs which she liked. When *Munbae Va En Anbae Va* played, his memories went back to the intimate day they had spent before she left. From somewhere, he was able to smell her deodorant. The previous day, after they had visited the museum and were returning to the hostel, as she rode pillion she asked him what the next plan of action was. He said he had no plans except to return to the hostel. "Take me somewhere where it is safe," she said.

"Where?"

"Anywhere you wish to take me."

"Can we go to the broken bridge?" he asked.

She felt this guy would never pick up her cues. "Come with me to my friend's room. Is that okay with you?" she asked.

He nodded. They both went to her friend's room. Her friend said she had some errands to run and left. The moment she left, she closed the door, hugged him tight and kissed him insanely. She bit him on his neck. She was out of control. She was hornier at certain times of the month and it was one of those days. He became breathless; he never thought she would be so passionate.

He slipped his hands underneath her t-shirt. His palms weren't sufficient to hold the fullness of her bosoms. His passion was like a sudden volcanic eruption. He bit on her bosom. Only then did he realise he enjoyed inflicting such pain; it sexually aroused him. He became like a Musth male elephant. After a few hours of intense foreplay, they had sex.

The clock ticked 12:00 a.m. on November 13. She received a Whatsapp message that wished her for her birthday. She thought he would call. She was very angry with him. She tried calling him but his mobile was switched off.

It was 6:00 a.m. when she received a voice message asking her to come to the park near her house. She woke up, got dressed and ran there. The sound of chirping birds, the scent of the plants around her and the drizzling rain aroused her mood. Vivian stood there in front of her. She ran and hugged him and said there could be no better birthday gift than his presence. She pointed to the love bite on his neck and professed her love for him. He kissed her on her forehead, gave her a bunch of red roses, got down on one knee and asked her if she would marry him. Tears started rolling down her cheeks.

Suddenly, her mobile phone rang and she was jolted from sleep. It was 6:00 a.m. All this while, she had been dreaming, but her eyes were still wet.

It was a call from Vivian. "Hi Vivian," she said, but someone else was on the other end. A mature, husky, authoritative male voice spoke in a different dialect of Tamil. "May I know who this is," he asked.

"Why?"

"Because yours was the last number dialled from this mobile."

"I'm Vivian's girlfriend…"

He told her he was calling from the local police station. He declared point blank that Vivian had died in a traffic accident the previous night. She became mute. Everything froze around her. Her breath stopped after a few seconds. There was a huge sigh followed by a thunderous outburst of tears. She threw her mobile. As it fell down she heard Vivian's voice in a video message. He had said the same things that she had dreamed of. Vivian was no more; she remembered the *Indian prayer* that Vivian liked.

When I am dead,

Cry for me a little,

Think of me sometimes,

But not too much.

Think of me now and again,

As I was in life.

At some moments it's pleasant to recall,

But not for long.

Leave me in peace,

And I shall leave you in peace.

And while you live,

Let your thoughts be with the living.

The Girl on the Other End

Everyone receives a call from some unidentified number every day. Some request sponsorships for the needy, and others are sales calls, but most such phone calls are a nuisance. It was a hot summer afternoon. Amidst the heavy traffic, he navigated through the busy roads in Chennai. The previous night, drink had made him sober. It had become a habit for him to drink heavily every other day. He had a vague memory of a cab driver to whom he had spoken in a local bar last night. The driver had complemented him on his English-speaking skills.

He was a postgraduate in science but no company was willing to give him a job. He searched for vacancies on every search portal and found a vacancy in an insurance company. This job meant a lot to him. He had to take care of his wife who was diagnosed with Tethered Cord Syndrome. She was wheelchair-bound and smelled of urine. All that he wanted was to be a noble husband. Though he was an afficionado of Dravidian philosophy his name sounded more bharaminic. The human resource manager of the insurance company sounded amiable. He assured him the job of a medical insurance counsellor.

On the day of his interview, he carried a file full of academic certificates and sports certificates which showcased his efficiency. However, none of the recruiters had even glimpsed at his file. Every recruiter expected some kind of influential recommendation. The HR agent of the insurance company was quite different. He was promising and skilled at recognising talent.

He parked his two-wheeler in the parking lot, wiped his sweat and groomed himself to be presentable. He entered the building complex of the insurance company. The HR department was on the third floor. The elevator wasn't working, and his hangover messed up his system. He had to climb three floors. He panted, began breathing like a dog and started sweating. The HR agent was waiting for him. He was extremely warm and well-mannered.

"Hi, I went through your profile. You seem to be extremely talented and I'm sure you will be an asset to our company," the agent said.

After two years of joblessness his words reassured him.

"Our boss is on leave today. You will probably have a personal interview with him tomorrow. Before that, I would like you to fill out this form as it's part of company procedure."

"Sure."

The form had basic information and academic details. There were three columns which insisted on religion, caste and community. He was an agnostic and secularist. He refuted discrimination based on religion and caste. He marked NIL in those columns, and handed over the form to the HR agent. The HR agent read the form and reacted.

"You haven't filled the columns on religion and caste?" he questioned.

"Is it mandatory to know my caste and religion before giving me a job? How does this matter to the company?"

Suddenly, the cordial HR agent turned disagreeable. His voice sounded different. Probably, he had misjudged him based on his bharaminic name.

"Well, we'll get back to you," said the HR agent.

He had no regrets about losing this opportunity. He wouldn't have been comfortable working under a casteist boss, he felt.

The next day, he spent time in a public park in the afternoon. This had been his routine for the past two years. Public parks were open till 9:00 a.m. in the mornings but in the afternoon, people used to trespass. He used to witness several characters trespass. Some people had team meetings, some found shelter under a tree to have their lunch, some young lovers found refuge amidst the greenery. One person was unique; he had dressed up in a bright yellow shirt and a red pair of pants. He wore make-up like an ace Tamil cine star.

He received phone calls on his mobile now and then. Some requested for credit cards and others for personal loans. He received one call from a service provider. The girl on the other end was very warm. Her voice was formal and respectful. But it sounded nostalgic to him. He was reminded of his ex-girlfriend. He wanted to hear her voice for some more time. He felt as though his broken relationship had been renewed.

"Sir...Sir..." she called.

He was jolted out of a pleasant dream. "Yes, madam, your voice sounds familiar to me. May I know your good name?" He asked.

"Sorry, Sir, our company policy doesn't allow me to reveal my name. Do you have any other questions, Sir?"

He felt ashamed for acting foolish. "Nothing, Madam. Sorry about that question."

She hung up.

He felt bad. A few moments later, he received a call from an anonymous number.

"Hi," said the girl on the other side. It was the same voice. Now, the voice sounded friendly and approachable. "My name is Meera. I also found your voice to be pleasing and caring," she said.

"Hi, Meera. Your voice sounded just like that of my ex-girlfriend. I was taken back to the beautiful memories of her," he said.

"Oh, okay, where is she now?"

"She is married and has settled down abroad. We separated mutually for practical reasons."

"Sorry to hear this...so, how long have you been working with this company?"

"It's been a while. I'm a science graduate. I had to take up this job for financial reasons."

"I talk to hundreds of customers on the phone every day. Your call was unique and was a surprise to me. It's very rare to see people who empathise these days. Even psychological emotions have transformed into digital emojis. I just felt like talking to you," she said.

Meera was an expert in recognising voice and tonal variations. She could identify even a mild mood change based on the tone of the speaker. She started talking to him daily from different numbers, mostly from public telephone booths. Some days, he would hear suburban railway announcements, and on others, the background sounds of a public transport bus. Some days, he could visualise a congested marketplace from her phone calls.

He requested her mobile number several times but she blankly refused to share it with him. It had become a habit for him to wait for her phone call every day. One day, he did not receive any phone call from her. He desperately checked his phone often. He was not able to comprehend his emotions. They were new to him. After his ex-girlfriend had walked out of his life and gotten married, he had never had such feelings for anyone. He felt it was immoral to talk to some stranger but his morality behaved like a monkey. He felt that humans were still uncivilised within.

The whole day went by without any call from her. He felt as though he was carrying a huge load on his chest. His emotions were inexplicable to him. At 3:00 p.m. the following day, he was at the public park, as usual, witnessing the routine happenings. He received a call but this time it was from a different caller from the same company.

He wanted to ask the caller about Meera but something stopped him from doing so.

After four days, he received a call from her. He was silent, he didn't respond to her words. She apologised for her behaviour. He was angry. He knew that anger was meant to be shown to one who would recognise it and appreciate the love behind it.

"I want to meet you," he said.

"Hmmm, when?" she asked.

"Tomorrow, at 2:00 p.m."

"Where?"

"The public park near the crossroads."

"Let me see, I can't promise you anything," Meera said.

"If you aren't coming, don't call me anymore. Get lost and don't ever call me," he said. He wasn't sure what he expected from Meera; an extramarital relationship or a plutonic friendship or just companionship.

"How do I recognise you?" questioned Meera.

"I will wear a black, crewneck t-shirt," he said.

"Okay, I'll meet you tomorrow," she said.

The following day, the public park was busy. There was a community art exhibition at the park. There were too many people there. Meera came dressed in a faded yellow top. She was not groomed well. Her teeth were crowded and crooked. She was dark-skinned. Her voice was a literal mismatch to her appearance. She never knew why she had accepted the invitation to meet him. There was a glimpse of love that she was able to sense. She was eager to meet him. She found him sitting on a stone bench. He was smart, clean-shaven and well-groomed. He wore a black, crewneck t-shirt.

Next to him, there was another person who also wore a black t-shirt with the image of Che Guevara on it. She wondered whom to approach. Her heart was thumping. She gathered all her courage and went near him.

"Hi," she said.

He was perplexed and reacted oddly.

"I'm Meera," she said.

"Sorry, I'm afraid that I don't know you," he said.

"Sorry for disturbing you. I mistook you to be someone I knew," said Meera. She walked away with tears rolling down her cheeks. She knew from his voice and tone that it was him.

He pretended to not recognise her. He was not able to accept her unattractiveness. He felt he was not the person he thought he was. Even he discriminated against people based on their appearance. He was no different from a casteist. He cringed thinking of his behaviour. His version of his personality was shameful to him.

Meera went to the root cause and found that he alone was at fault. Her love persisted in the mind of her client whom she called every day.

Calcutta's Old Flame

It was November 2001. He never knew why she had insisted on him coming to Calcutta. That was how Kolkata was called in those days. It was too short of a notice to get a train ticket. He found a ticket agent and paid huge money to get a ticket. The ticket was waitlisted as 151. Travelling to Calcutta from Chennai on a train is a tedious journey.

He was able to see people swarming around the TTE for their tickets to be confirmed. His chance of getting his berth for the long-distance journey was minimal. Somehow, he got a seat near the window. The Howrah Express left Chennai at 10:30 p.m. It took a while for the pandemonium inside the compartment to settle down. It was the first time he was travelling to Calcutta all alone. In those days, they had to carry several audio compact cassettes to enjoy music during travel with a Walkman.

There was a north Indian family which occupied the bogie near him. They were busy eating their dinner. The smell of the pickle was all around. The aroma of the pickle and the odour of urine from the toilet created a disgusting and nauseating feeling. Most of them in the compartment spoke in Hindi or Bengali. He felt like an alien in the train. His sole companion was the music from a Tamil film; one specific song of AR Rahman which he played in a loop. He had to wait until the Walkman completed rewinding. Shankar Mahadevan's song brought back nostalgic memories with his friend.

She was his good friend. They had spent several moments together. Both were postgraduate medical students in Bombay, which is now called Mumbai. There were several days where they used to chat for long hours. Some days, they used to spend talking sweet nothings, sitting on the pavement near Haji Ali beach in Mumbai. It was always a delight to witness Haji Dargah on a full moon night. The yellow rays of the halogen street lights, the flashing car lights, the decorated lights of the Dargah and its reflection in the sea... all these scenes were a photographer's delight. Some days, she used to teach statistics while taking a stroll along the sea. It was the wrong place to learn statistics though.

She was a gorgeous girl. Any man would dream of a girl with such expertise in arithmetic. She was soon to be married after postgraduation;

her parents desperately searched for a groom. Some days, the prospective groom's family would pay her a visit at the hostel. She was open-minded and agreeable to any groom of her parents' choice. All that she wanted was a level-headed person. She understood that marriage was both a commitment and compromise. She was a high-spirited girl and never had he seen her in a dull, sober mood. He never understood how a girl would be without any mood swings, even on rare occasions.

They stayed in opposite hostel rooms on the third floor of the same building. There were no intercoms or mobile phones to communicate in those days. I really wondered how they managed to communicate. They used to pre-plan their time together and if either one of them didn't turn up, each had the patience to wait till the other came.

The ticket examiner touched his shoulder and interrupted his trail of past memories. He told him that there was one upper berth in the next compartment. Would he be interested in moving there? Dev retrieved Rs 200 from his wallet to show the TTE his gratitude for offering him the upper berth. The upper berth was a luxury to Dev. It offered a birds eye view of the happenings in the compartment in the moving train. Eating and sleeping happened in repeat cycles without disturbing co-passengers. He settled in the upper berth. The compartment's cacophony slowly faded and the chugging sounds were hypnotising. The past flashed before his eyes again.

It was February, 2001. Dev and his college batchmates were travelling in a train for a medical conference in Delhi. Loads of chitchatting and gossiping took place among friends. A few of them played cards.

Dev and shruti sat opposite each other on the side RAC seats. Their legs were stretched out underneath a quilt. The cold breeze blew through the lower part of the shutter window as it had not been closed properly. He was able to feel the warmth of her thighs through her tight denim jeans. She was wearing a red, checked, cotton shirt; her beauty was irresistible. Dev wore a white, round neck t-shirt with the words 'The Terry Fox Run – 2000' printed on it.

It was 11:55 p.m. Almost everyone was fast asleep. Both of them were still awake chatting about sweet nothings. Suddenly, she got up from her seat to get something from her hand bag. He wondered what she was trying to do when she retrieved a greeting card from it and gave it to him. It said, Happy Valentine's Day.

"Am I your boyfriend?" Dev asked.

"You need not be in love with someone to celebrate Valentine's Day. Even a dear friend can be your Valentine," she said.

He was puzzled and asked himself, then why do we celebrate Friendship Day? While reminiscing, Dev fell asleep. The next morning, he got up early to take care of his daily ablutions. Long-distance trains were exciting. You are witness to different people, different behaviours, different languages, different socioeconomic classes and different styles of dressing. Dev's diet on the train was confined to bread and omelette sold on the platform as it was affordable and tasted the same across the country. He kept himself occupied reading *Wings of Fire.*

The train reached Kharkpur junction, which is considered to be the world's third longest platform. It was 1:52 a.m. The train was on time. There was a five-minute halt at the Kharkpur junction. He got down on the platform; the junction was deserted. There was a chai wala from whom he bought a cup of chai. Tea served in mud cups was a delight to drink. Before the chai wala returned his change, the train started moving.

Dev was half asleep on the upper berth, still wondering why she had insisted that he come to Kolkata. The last time they had spoken over an

STD phone call, she told him that there was a groom who had seen her recently and the match would most likely be finalized. He had received this call while he was watching a Tamil film late at night in a cinema hall. After talking to her, he felt disturbed. Something was bothering him and he was not able to understand this inexplicable emotion.

Time had literally come to a standstill. It had already been thirty hours of travel. It moved at a slow pace. He did not know how to speed up the passage of time. He was not able to sleep. He switched on the Walkman and played Kenny G's album *Breathless*. Suddenly, there was a lot of commotion in the compartment. The train had reached Howrah junction. The time was around 4:15 a.m. Thank God he had been disturbed by the chaos, otherwise he would have continued sleeping. The station was still not active with its usual hustle and bustle.

He got down from the train and waited on the platform. He did not know what to do. He had noted her address and phone number on a piece of paper which he had kept in his wallet. He thought to call her but it was too early to disturb her. Suddenly, someone rushed towards him. It was a great relief to see her.

Shruthi had come with her father to receive him. She shook her hands and said, welcome to Calcutta. She was a Tamilian born and brought up in Calcutta. She wore a faded cotton, crimson red churidar. She said, "Hi Dev." That's how she used to call him. He liked the way she addressed him. Once in a while she would call him fatty which would annoy him. She introduced him to her father. He was very friendly and jovial.

Her house was nearly thirty kilometres away from Howrah. They booked a cab after her father had succeeded in bargaining a reasonable fare. Her father was a gentleman. He sat next to the driver and she sat next to him. She held his hand and said, "I missed you." He didn't know how to react in front of her father. He just reciprocated with a smile. They travelled in a cab; it was an old Ambassador painted in a deep yellow. Bengali drivers are known for rash driving. Her father asked him to slow down and pay attention to the road.

Shruti and Dev sat in the back seat. She said to him, "Thanks for coming". Her eyes longed to tell a tale. Dev was still not able to figure out why she had asked him to come. She had blocked a room for him in a mansion. The cab decelerated and turned into a narrow street where there was an old mansion. It was a ramshackle cottage. He shared the room with an old, grey-haired fragile man. He looked like an energy sucker. He sounded like a dejected, lost person. The thought of spending the next three nights in this mansion was harrowing.

It was 9:30 a.m. She returned to the mansion with a friend. They had breakfast on the streets of Calcutta. The street food was mouth-watering and sumptuous. The following night, she insisted that he stay in her flat. She took him to their single bedroom flat in the Salt Lake area. Her single bedroom flat was very organised and clean. There was an old Dyanora black and white television in the corner. The TV screamed the news in Bengali early in the morning.

Her family was well-organised and everything was systematic. They had dinner at 7:30 p.m. and went to bed at 9:00 p.m. sharp. These rules were a bit weird and uncomfortable for Dev to follow. That night, he was unable to sleep. He suffered from sleep paralysis in a new environment. The Hag effect haunted him. It was pitch dark sporadically. The darkness was interspersed with light thanks to the moving traffic. It was midnight. Her father was fast asleep. He snored loudly and his breath paused now and then. Shruthi went to him, pulled his quilt over him and kissed him on his forehead thinking that he was asleep. He held her hand for a moment. There was a spark of light which illuminated his thoughts. "Are you still awake?" she asked.

"Hmm…unable to sleep."

Shruti's mother was shrewd. She saw him as a predator in the house trying to conquer her daughter. Shruti had different plans in her mind. She had a week-long schedule for him in Kolkata. Shruti was a strict vegetarian. She even felt nauseous at the smell of garlic and onions. In contrast, he was strictly non-vegetarian. She wanted him to enjoy the street foods of Calcutta, those egg rolls, chicken wraps and puchkas. She wanted him to taste the black forest pastries at Monginis cake shop.

He still never understood why she had invited him to Calcutta. He never asked her the reason, he just went with the flow. It was his second day in Calcutta. He went with her parents for a morning stroll. The chillness of the November air, the aroma of charcoal stoves from street tea shops, and the chirping birds boosted his serotonin levels. He had never felt happier.

Shruti told him about her marriage plans and the prospective grooms who had come to see her. She recollected the days spent in Mumbai with him. Shruti's father interrupted. "What about visiting the Victoria Memorial today?" he asked. She told him that they had different plans and asked him to carry on with his routine work. Her father was married to his desk; he was a workaholic. Her mother worked as a lecturer in a college.

It was 9:30 a.m. Suddenly, her father felt sick and had a panic attack. He started sweating profusely. Shruti was worried. She comforted him and took him to a nearby hospital. Dev accompanied them. His BP had shot up marginally. There was nothing serious to worry about, declared the duty doctor.

After everything had settled, she took him to a Hindi movie called *Abhay,* which portrayed Kamal Hassan as a schizophrenic patient. The interlude of animation in the film was innovative and creative, he thought, being a movie buff. The warmth of the beautiful girl sitting next to him was a major distraction. She was dressed in a white top and her small, black *bindi* was like the full stop at the end of well-written poetry.

Later, she took him to Azhad Dhaba at Ballygunge Circular Road. It was a small, forty-seat dhaba. After they had ordered vegetarian Hakka noodles, she told him to turn around. It was a pleasant surprise. Dev saw an original painting done by the great master, M.F. Hussain. It was like witnessing Da Vinci's Salvator Mundi. He was speechless and mesmerised. What more could this trip to Calcutta offer, he thought? But there was a much bigger surprise that awaited him.

There was one last day in Calcutta. He had tickets reserved in The Coromandel Express. He still had no clue as to why he had been invited to Calcutta. He didn't know why he had accepted Shruti's invitation. That evening, she took him to Millennium Park located on the eastern banks of the Huguli river. It was dark. The reflection of the ferry lights and the Howrah Bridge was captivating. She didn't speak to him for a while; she sat alone. Dev enjoyed the night sky and the beauty of the Huguli River.

She came close to him, held his hand, looked into his eyes and said, "Dev…I think I should get married to you."

He was silent for a while. "Are you in love with me?" he asked. "Can you just say it once?" he added.

"Say what?"

"Tell me that you love me."

"Certain things are better left unsaid," she said. "Talk to my parents," she added.

The following morning, when they were on their morning walk, Dev gathered all his courage and asked her father for his daughter's hand.

His face changed. "If this is what she wants, she is free to go with you under one condition; she must forget about us. She cannot have a relationship with us. Though the world has changed, caste, colour and creed still matter. We are ordinary people. We won't risk antagonising the society we live in."

Tears rolled down Dev's cheeks. He didn't speak a word. Shruti was inquisitive to know what had happened. She pestered him for the details. "I can't replace your parents. Let us be special friends," he said. The rest of the day was painful.

The next day, he was all set to leave Calcutta. Shruti wanted to go with him to the station, but her mother was against it. She said that she would accompany them. She had booked a cab to the Howrah Station. The cab was waiting. Her mother went downstairs. A few minutes later, Dev and Shruti followed. On the staircase, Shruti pulled Dev closer and kissed him passionately. "I can never remove you from my thoughts. I will always miss you," she said. Her eyes were filled with tears. She held his hand tight. "Dev, remember, we can never be happy if we want to keep others happy. With your permission, let us bury our desires and part ways. I'm extremely sorry for causing you any inconvenience by coming into your life."

Both of them mutually consented to keep others happy. As he walked down the stairs, he saw a picture of Mahatma Gandhi hanging on the wall and remembered his quote: There are no goodbyes for us. Wherever you are, you will always be in my heart.

Director's Cut...

Aaryan was an aspiring film director, passionate about movie-making. He had never had the opportunity to work as an assistant to any director in the movie industry. Books by Seinfeld and the Five C's of cinematography helped him learn the craft a little.

There was a state-level short film competition which was a ticket to the mainstream film industry. Aaryan wanted to direct a film which was hard-hitting and would grab the attention of the panel of judges. Suffering from a creative block, he was not able to conceive any concepts for a short film. He was frustrated. Time was running out. There was just one last day to submit the entry for the competition.

Years back, when he was a lecturer in an engineering college, he had had a relationship with his student. Her name was Diya. She was a tall, thin girl whose intelligence attracted him. She was assertive and straightforward. He never knew that he was her favourite teacher. Every director loots their first script from personal experiences and true stories. Aaryan tried to do the same. He travelled through his past memories to freeze a fragment and turn it into visual drama.

It was a Sunday afternoon. Most often, Sundays made him lose his sanity due to boredom. He pitched a few ideas for the short film to his assistant director, Kavya. Kavya was a feminist; she was an unusual woman who didn't fit the conventional mould of womanhood. She was a silent admirer of Aaryan. They were both immersed in discussing possibilities for the short film while drinking liquor. Kavya fiercely competed with any man when it came to alcohol. Her favourite drink was black rum mixed with cola.

Aaryan pitched an incident pertaining to his relationship with Diya. Aaryan was an artist to; he painted portraits and surrealist painting meticulously. Most of his painting portrayed pain and agony. The choice of colour, the theme, every inch of the canvas were filled with enormous anguish. Diya was an aesthete; she visited his house to see his art works. She looked attractive in a lemon-yellow churidar. Her dangling earrings added to her beauty. She had loads of admiration for her lecturer. She was not just intellectually but also sexually attracted to him. She lost herself and went into a trance admiring his artwork. She noticed a commonality in every work of his. She wanted to see more energy and happiness in his works.

"Sir, can you paint something very colourful and happy? I see a lot of pain in your works. I want to see something happy. Can you do it for me?" she requested.

Aryan took a charcoal stick and his sketch book to draw something which Diya would perceive to be happy. He failed in his attempts.

"It's just like you. You are not getting it, Sir," she said.

"Paintings are an expression of the mind; it is a spontaneous portrayal of past experiences and the state of the mind. Your painting is a narrative of your painful past. Redraw some happy moments on your canvas. Analyse yourself. Don't bury your happiness in your past. Live the moment and live for yourself," Diya added.

She was very mature for her age, he thought.

"What would make you happy?" she asked. She held his hands and kissed him. Tears rolled down Aaryan's face. He cried his heart out. She hugged him. "Hey, stop crying and start living," she told him. His hands trembled and were desperate to caress the firmness of her bosom. His hands wandered over her lemon-yellow churidar top.

She allowed him no time to hesitate or feel guilty. His hands were stained with graphite. She held his hands and placed them on her bosom. "Do whatever you want with me. I'm yours, but make sure that your next painting portrays abundant happiness," she told him.

Diya's lemon-yellow churidar was soiled with black stains from Aryan's hands. The charcoal stains revealed an aggressive passion that formed a deep, dark impression on her clothes. Kavya was literally blown away by his arousing narration. Her nipples became hard and started protruding through her tight brassiere. She interrupted to ask, "Can I pour you another glass of whiskey?" She saw him break while he narrated the incident. She asked, "Do you still love her?"

There were moments of silence. "Humans can never forget anything. They may pretend to have forgotten. Even time doesn't heal certain things. Moreover, I'm perfectly happy being unhappy," he said. "I still keep sending Diya emails knowing that I will not receive a reply. I know she's married and it's wrong on my part to expect reciprocation from her side, but still, human emotion fails to understand the virtues of society. I long for her love," he added.

Women don't understand that love is beyond sex and not every man can pretend to love just to have sex.

"I still love her," he declared.

The following day, he had a severe hangover. He tried to figure out what he had conceived as a script for his short film. "How are you going to develop the script with this minuscule incident?" Kavya asked.

"Give me two days, I will give you the bound script for your review," he said.

Two days passed by. He gave her the bound script for her to read and refine it.

Kavya read the script except for the incident which he had shared with her earlier. The character resembled her more than Diya. Line by line, there was love and passion. She was not able to put the bound script down even for a second. She was dumbstruck! She wondered about Aaryan's observation and narrative. He had recounted even trivial things. The whole script looked like a work of nonfiction rather than fiction to her.

That night, he called her. "Did you read my script?" he asked.

"Yes."

"How was it?"

"I have no words…"

"Do you want me to refine it further or do you have any suggestions?" he asked.

"Can I write the dialogues?" she asked.

"I would love that."

Days rolled by with preproduction work, shooting and post production work. They were working on the dubbing session. Aaryan was not convinced with the female lead voice. She wasn't getting the right modulation and was not living the character. He noticed Kavya tutoring the female lead to dub.

"Hey, Kavya, you better do it yourself; you sound more realistic and you can do justice to the character," he said.

After the sound-mixing and special-effects work, the film was completed and ready for the competition. Their film was one among three selected for the final round. The grand finale was held in the presence of top directors in the field. The screening was scheduled in the evening. The auditorium had a huge screen, where the films would be screened. Aaryan and Kavya found it very difficult to find their seats. There were several celebrities in attendance. The laser light projection on the stage danced to the tunes of high energy music. The show started and all the films were screened one after the other.

Aaryan's film was ready to be screened. The anchor announced the film's name. Kavya sat at the edge of her seat biting her nails. The moment Aaryan saw his name on the big screen for the first time, his heart felt like it was about to burst, unable contain the joy. Later, the judges talked about the pros and cons of each film before announcing the first prize. The first two places were announced and their film hadn't made it. After much negative criticism, Aaryan's film was given the third place.

He was happy and felt that it was a real learning experience. As he walked off the stage, someone called out to him. He introduced himself as an entrepreneur and a movie buff. He retrieved a cheque book from his blazer pocket and signed a cheque for Rs 5 lakh. "I liked your film and you are going to direct my next film," he said. Aaryan froze for a moment; he was not able to believe what had just happened. The producer said he was able to feel a sense of reality and true emotion in his film. Aaryan was at the right place at the right moment.

A few days later, Kavya was not able continue as his AD due to health reasons. Aaryan was busy refining and rewriting his short film for the big screen. He wanted to make the climax very gripping. To make it hard-hitting he laced the plot with a fictitious climax. The female lead would be diagnosed with end stage carcinoma. He wanted to get Kavya's feedback and called her mobile. His call was not answered. After a few attempts, Kavya picked up his call.

"Hey, how are you? Are you okay?" he asked.

"I am undergoing my third chemo cycle," she said.

One Rupee Water Packet

It was not just another day for Magizhan. He was a simple, boy-next-door kind of guy with unusual goals in his life. He was not like other stereotypical personalities who aimed for big salaries and a comfortable life. He had transformed into the person he was because of the books he had read and the people he had met. Karl Marx, Hegel, Che Guevara and Fidel Castro influenced him a lot. He had met his girlfriend in a political meeting and their relationship was going steady. Magizhan's way of life and his ideologies were intolerable to his father who was a businessman. He put up with him for a long time and one fine day he threw him out of his house.

The next day was very painful for him. He was clueless about his next steps. He did not know what to do with his life. He just had Rs 100 with him. He felt desolate and miserable. Even the sweltering Chennai summer heat didn't burn him much. He was lost and wandered like a nomad on the streets of Chennai. He decided to meet a comrade who lived on the outskirts of Chennai. He went to the Chennai suburban terminal at Moore Market complex to take a train to Pattabiram. He was hungry and he hadn't had breakfast.

He heard muffled voices in his head. His head felt heavy. The temperature in his head was more than the heat of the summer sun. He stretched his Rs 100 note into the ticket window to buy a ticket. The booking clerk was sweating and looked very irritable. He yelled at him in Tamil for not rendering the exact change for the ticket. Magizhan was not in a state to retaliate. He just apologized and sulked.

He had lived a comfortable life with his father's earnings. He had lived in an air-conditioned room with loads of books, a laptop and compact discs scattered and unorganized on his bed, until the previous night. His father had provided a lavish life for his single son. The conspiracy of his father's concubine made his father disown him.

He just had Rs 90 left. His mobile phone was drained of charge. His girlfriend called him. He narrated what happened. He was in no mood to get her help. "What are you going to do?" she asked.

"I don't know," came the blunt reply. She was able to sense how he felt from the way he sounded. "My home is no more my destination," he said, his voice choking.

"Hey, are you okay? Don't give up, stay strong," she encouraged.

"I don't know when I will call you again. Until then, goodbye."

Before she could react, he hung up.

He had random thoughts. Sometimes, when we don't intend to change, time takes a hold of us. It might be fate or destiny. Whether you like it or not, time will sculpt you to meet your life's needs. Everything that happens in life has a purpose. When life takes you on a rollercoaster ride, you are not able to comprehend why miserable incidents happen, initially. But later, you will be able to connect the dots.

The public address system announced that the train departing to Kumudipoondi would leave from Platform 6 in a while. He walked towards the train. Even his walk projected his state of mind. It was slow paced and lacked energy, He got into the train. The compartment was occupied by various characters. Everyone seemed to be happy, according to him.

Unlike the Mumbai suburban trains, Chennai trains were less crowded. That day, it was less crowded as well. Some college girls in their hijabs mumbled in Urdu. A few male students tried to grab the attention of girls in the compartment. A few passengers were reading Tamil newspapers. There were transgenders in the train too. He failed to get a seat. He was already worn-out and hungry. His trauma was killing him. He just held the centre bar at the entrance of the compartment. For a second, he felt like throwing himself out of the running train and killing himself.

The trained reached Perambur station. A twelve-year-old boy, who was dark-skinned, thin and very energetic, with sacred ash on his forehead, entered the train with a small jute sack full of ice water packets on his shoulder. He barged into the compartment shouting, 'ice water, ice water.' Drinking water had also become a commodity of luxury; nothing was free of cost.

To quench their thirst in the hot summer, everyone in the compartment who could afford it bought water packets. Most of the water packet were sold. There were around ten to twelve ice water packets left in the bundle. The boy carried the sack on his left shoulder.

He had a stack of one-rupee coins in his right palm. He held these coins carefully inside the palm of his hand without dropping them due to the oscillation of the train.

He came near the entrance of the compartment, leaned over and supported his back with his legs spread apart to increase the base of support to avoid falling and started counting the stalk of coins in his hand. The sun's rays fell directly on his face, but his attention was not distorted a bit. He moved each coin meticulously to count the total number of water packets sold.

Suddenly, the boy had hiccups. The hiccups worsened and it continued. Magizhan curiously watched the boy, wondering what he was doing. He wondered if stress and depression hormones had a direct link with the creative brain. A blind person selling ballpoint pens suddenly crossed his path and interrupted his observation. The hiccups hadn't stopped, they persisted. He hoped to drink some water to stop hiccupping. He touched the ice water packets left in the sack. His hiccups forced him to drink a sachet of water.

The train slowed down. It had reached Hindu College station. It came to a screeching halt. A water tap appeared directly at the entrance of the train. The water was dripping as the tap hadn't been closed properly. The boy put his coins into his pant pocket and rushed towards the tap. He gulped the water from the tap and closed the tap properly without wasting the precious water. The hiccups stopped. Then he disappeared off into the crowd on the station platform.

Magizhan felt that this episode was trying to teach him something. When he had surplus money, he had plenty of friends around and had great parties. He lived a life of extravagance. He never thought of saving a single penny for his future. Just because his father was frugal, sacrificed his good times, didn't buy the things he wanted, Magizhan had enjoyed his savings. This habit which he had acquired in his adolescence, was difficult to shake.

A single rupee was important to the boy who sold water packets despite his persistent hiccups. He could have easily ceased his hiccups by drinking the leftover water packets, but he didn't do so. Why wasn't he like the little boy? This question hit him hard. This incident was a starting point for him. He started his life from here. He just had Rs 98 when he was stranded on the road but this incident made him develop 100 percent positivity. That one-rupee water packet was not the end of the story but just the beginning for a great comrade in the making.

Stoned!

My room is a big-sized coffin, nailed on all sides. There is no way I can see the outer world. It is surrounded by darkness, the darkest darkness. I feel I am submerged in a pool of water; I hear strange sounds at regular intervals. I'm unable to make out the words; they are muffled. Am I in the womb or the primordial soup? What am I supposed to be? A Pisces or a Sapien?

I keep expecting a ray of light to seep through a metaphysical hole. There is no sense of time. There is no ticking of the clock. I can't hear the chirping birds, the hustle and bustle of traffic, the cry of a baby, the laughter of an adolescent and gossip amongst the oldies. I cannot sense the touch of another human. I can't smell the odour of her axilla. I can't experience an orgasm.

I see faint images of people coming to meet me in my dreams. Is it really my dream? They care for me; they take me for a stroll on the wet beach shore. I can't see the indentation of my foot on the surface of the sand. They ruminate about the old memories they shared with me. I am jolted forward. I start running naked on the deserted shore. A crowd waits to receive me with their arms wide open. I can barely recognise a few faces. Most of them are unfamiliar to me. Someone shouts in the crowd, telling me that he was my bloodline when the Pharaohs ruled.

Suddenly, I fall with a startle from a tall tree. I'm not sure what kind of tree it is. The fall is never-ending. I wait to reach the ground but it is an endless wait. The dream vanishes into smoke. I evolved and stopped sleeping on the trees two million years ago. How can I fall? Is it preserved in my double helix immortal coils?

I feel someone walking near my cot, someone sits next to me and caresses my chest. I'm powerless to feel the warmth of their palm. Instantly, I freeze, unable to move. My blood fails to circulate. I feel my body is bound to the bed. Someone sits on my chest and holds my arms and legs. I scream but my voice is inaudible. No one is alarmed by my scream. I struggle to release myself from the grip of an inexplicable animated figure. My struggle goes in vain.

How do I look? I'm unable to see myself. Do I look ugly or smart? On what scale should I measure myself if I'm unable to see myself? I search for a mirror in the darkness. What's the point? A mirror does not reflect without any light?

I hear some odd noise. Is it the bloodsucking insects that hover around my ears producing an annoying buzz or is it an old, broken transistor radio searching for the appropriate frequency?

My hands feel alien to me. Am I touching myself? There is a discordant transmission of neural impulse. My mouth isn't bitter due the lack of saliva. I want to crawl out of bed and creep up the wall in search of some sunlight. My vision fails to form images. My head feels empty without my sixty-thousand thoughts, my eyes fail to burn and my phallus slumbers.

Am I alive or dead? I am unable to sense my breath. I am unable to hear my snore and there is no one around me. Has my body become a decaying biological piece of junk or has it become cosmic dust? Where are my thoughts? Where is my intelligence? Where is my cognition? Has it all vanished in cortical shutdown or has it disappeared into the metaverse searching for an inhabitable planet where I can wake up from my own sleep in a body which is zillions of light years away from an incomprehensible parallel universe.

www.ingramcontent.com/pod-product-compliance
Lightning Source LLC
Chambersburg PA
CBHW022028150726
47990CB00002B/869